Traction Man
Is Here
MINI GREY

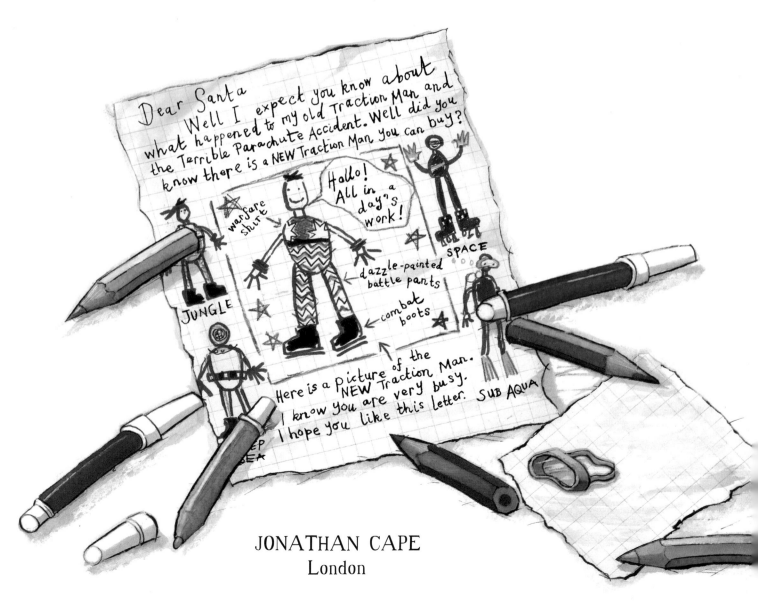

JONATHAN CAPE
London

Traction Man is here!
(Wearing Combat Boots, Battle Pants and his Warfare Shirt.)

Traction Man is guarding some toast.

He has volunteered for a Special Mission.

Traction Man is diving in the foamy waters
of the Sink (wearing his Sub-Aqua Suit,
Fluorescent Flippers and Infra-Red Mask).

He is searching for the
Lost Wreck of the Sieve.

"Well done,
Scrubbing Brush!
You can be my pet!"

Just ten minutes, remember...

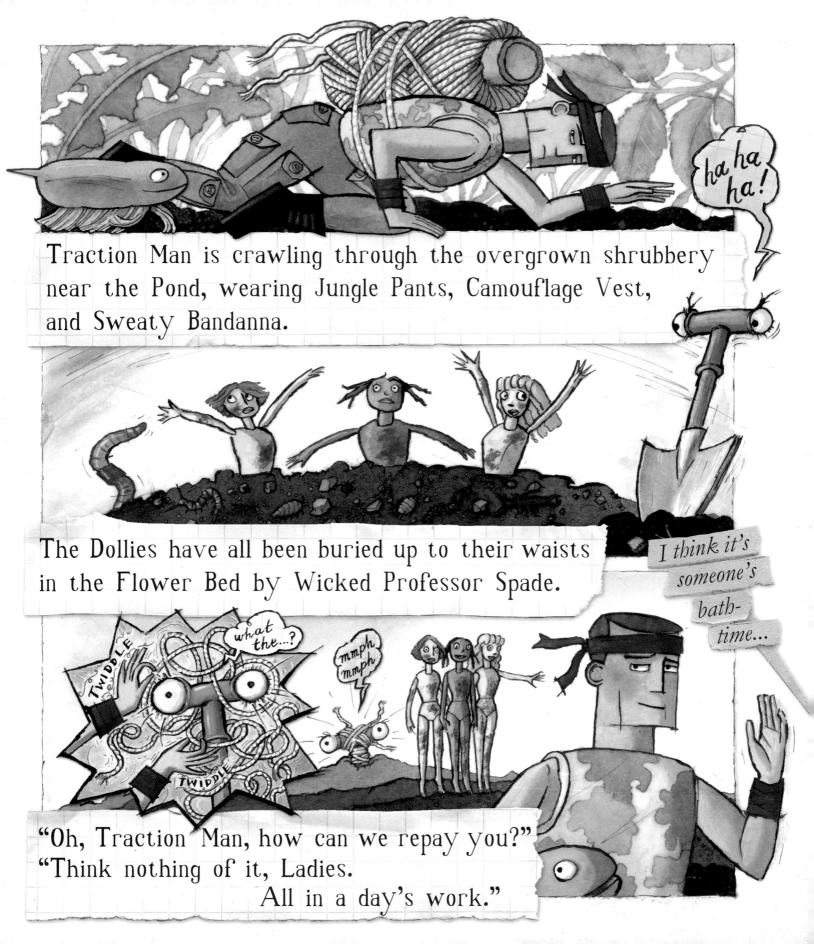

ha ha ha!

Traction Man is crawling through the overgrown shrubbery near the Pond, wearing Jungle Pants, Camouflage Vest, and Sweaty Bandanna.

I think it's someone's bath-time...

The Dollies have all been buried up to their waists in the Flower Bed by Wicked Professor Spade.

TWIDDLE

what the...?

TWIDDLE

mmph mmph

"Oh, Traction Man, how can we repay you?"
"Think nothing of it, Ladies.
                    All in a day's work."

Traction Man and Scrubbing Brush are in the Giant InterGalactic People Mover.

They are counting Christmas trees.

They are put into suspended animation for some of the journey.

At last!
Granny's!

Everyone has a present to open.
Even **Traction Man**.

Scrubbing Brush
is **very** excited.

Oh! How lovely.
An all-in-one knitted green romper suit
and matching bonnet!

"I knitted it myself," says Granny.
"It is special Traction Man green.
For jungles."

Oh, how nice.

Socks again.

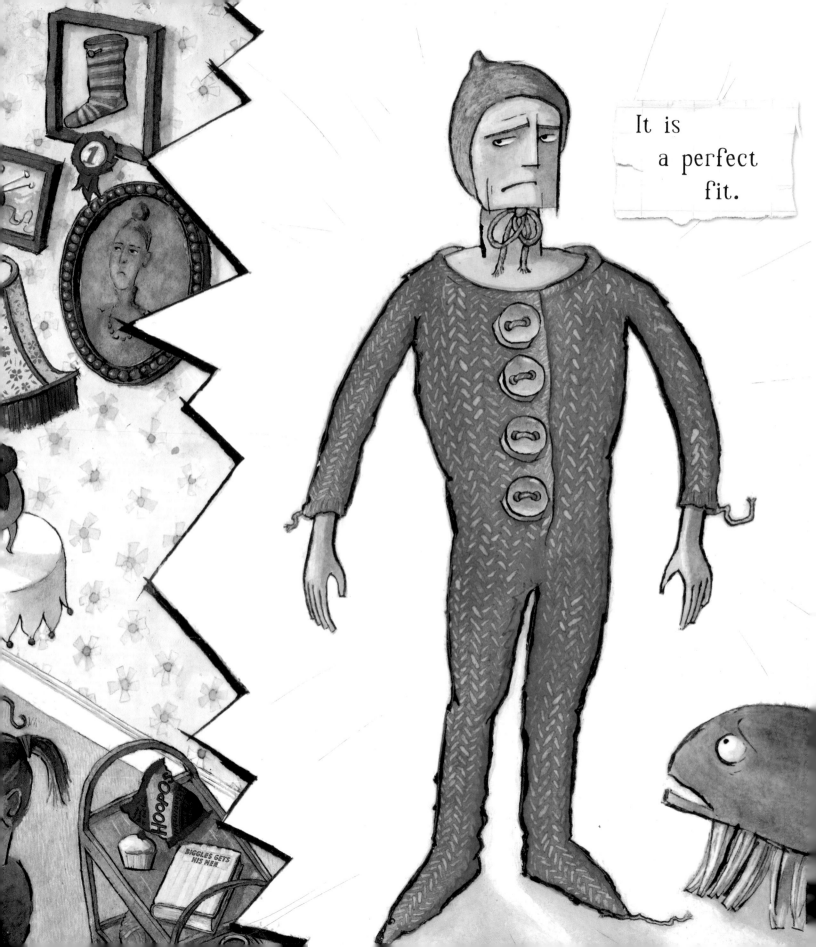

It is
a perfect
fit.

Traction Man is speeding in his **Supersonic Space-Cup** and **Saucer** (wearing his all-in-one knitted green romper suit and matching bonnet) on his way to rescue the Cupcake from the clutches of Doctor Sock.

But—
Oh no!

Well at least Scrubbing Brush doesn't laugh at him.

Traction Man is sitting on the edge of the Kitchen Cliff
(wearing an all-in-one knitted green romper suit
and matching bonnet).

Arf Arf Arf.

Arf!

Arf!

Arf!

Oh DO be quiet, Scrubbing Brush.

My Goodness! Down there!
All those spoons have crashed! They must be helped – but how? The Kitchen Cliff is **very** high.

Look at that dust cloud!
We must hurry!
The Broom
is coming!

What **IS** Scrubbing Brush doing?

Traction Man and **Scrubbing Brush**
are relaxing after their latest mission,
lying comfortably on a book
in the huge blue expanse
of the Carpet.

Traction Man is wearing his
knitted Green Swimming Pants
and matching Swimming Bonnet.

They are both wearing their medals.

And they know they are ready
for **Anything.**

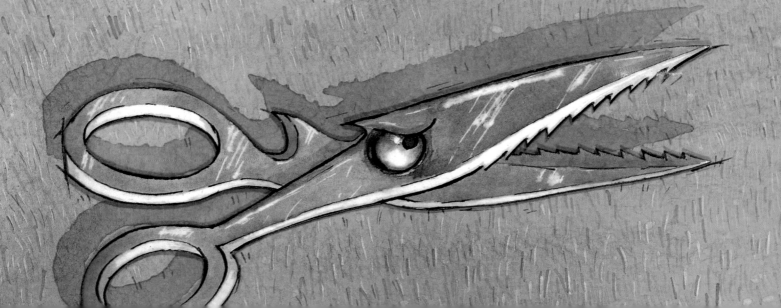

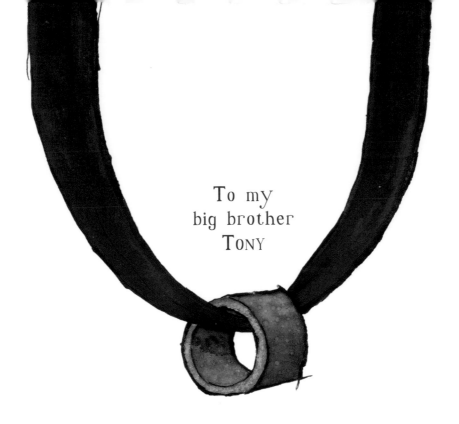

To my
big brother
TONY

TRACTION MAN IS HERE
A JONATHAN CAPE BOOK 0 224 06495 9

Published in Great Britain by Jonathan Cape,
an imprint of Random House Children's Books

This edition published 2005

1 3 5 7 9 10 8 6 4 2

Copyright © Mini Grey, 2005

The right of Mini Grey to be identified as the author
of this work has been asserted in accordance
with the Copyright, Designs and Patents Act 1988.

RANDOM HOUSE CHILDREN'S BOOKS
61–63 Uxbridge Road, London W5 5SA
A division of The Random House Group Ltd

RANDOM HOUSE AUSTRALIA (PTY) LTD
20 Alfred Street, Milsons Point, Sydney,
New South Wales 2061, Australia

RANDOM HOUSE NEW ZEALAND LTD
18 Poland Road, Glenfield, Auckland 10, New Zealand

RANDOM HOUSE (PTY) LTD
Endulini, 5A Jubilee Road, Parktown 2193, South Africa

THE RANDOM HOUSE GROUP Limited Reg. No. 954009
www.kidsatrandomhouse.co.uk

A CIP catalogue record for this book is available
from the British Library.

Printed and bound in Singapore